MONSTER HIGH™

Little Sister Stories

Fangelica's Batty Bake Club

MONSTER HIGH

Little Sister Stories
Fangelica's Batty Bake Club

SOPHIE FINN

Little, Brown and Company
New York ✳ Boston

MONSTER HIGH and associated trademarks are owned by and used under license from Mattel. © 2018 Mattel. All Rights Reserved.

Cover design by Véronique L. Sweet. Cover illustration by Melissa Manwill.

Little, Brown and Company
Hachette Book Group
1290 Avenue of the Americas, New York, NY 10104
Visit us at LBYR.com
monsterhigh.com

First Edition: July 2018

Little, Brown and Company is a division of Hachette Book Group, Inc. The Little, Brown name and logo are trademarks of Hachette Book Group, Inc.

The publisher is not responsible for websites (or their content) that are not owned by the publisher.

Library of Congress Control Number 2017960094

ISBN: 978-0-316-51262-6 (pbk.)

Printed in the United States of America

LSC-C

10 9 8 7 6 5 4 3 2 1

To Sloane and Jasper

CHAPTER 1

Fanging Out with Fangelica

The bell rings, which means it's time for class at Monster High. Ghouls stop at their coffin lockers to get their books. Mansters high-five one another. Deuce Gorgon and Skelly are talking about their band's new song. Lagoona Blue is excited about swim team practice that afternoon.

Fangelica Van Bat, Draculaura's adopted little sister, watches everyone stream past her. They are all busy! They all have so much to do.

Fangelica still isn't used to seeing so many different monsters! She's used to being the *only* monster around. Until just recently, she'd been on her own in the big, empty Van Bat castle. It was pretty lonely being the only vampire there.

I'm so lucky Draculaura decided to go on a monster mission to find me, thinks Fangelica. *Now when I bake chocolate crypt cookies, I can share them with my new vampire family.*

Just last night, Dracula and Draculaura watched the Normie movie *Dracula* together.

"Humans don't know anything about vampires." Draculaura giggled. "They think we're so scary!"

"As scary as me?" Fangelica asked her big

sister. She stuck some candy worms in her nose and made a silly face.

"My fangs!" Dracula and Draculaura exclaimed together.

"I love how goofy you are, Fangelica." Draculaura laughed.

Fangelica smiles. She's been having such an amazing time with her sister at Monster High! Fangelica and Draculaura do so many things together—from going on field trips by using the Mapalogue to practicing turning into bats and flying.

That's the best part about this school! Fangelica thinks. *Everybody here can be exactly who they are!* But Fangelica is not old enough to go to classes yet, and she's not old enough to join any of Monster High's many after-school clubs.

Where is Draculaura? Fangelica wonders.

She peers down the howlway and spots a friendly ghoul.

"Hi!" calls Fangelica to Ari Hauntington as she floats by. But the ghost ghoul is hurrying to her Haunting class and doesn't hear her.

Fangelica skips over to Cleo de Nile, her sister's friend. Fangelica's little pink bat wings flutter. Her dark curls bounce. But Cleo is rewrapping her bandages. She's too busy to talk to Fangelica too.

Dracula rushes by on his way to teach history class. Gob is skipping Mad Science to eat some more. He disappears around the corner on the way to the Creepeteria.

Fangelica peeks through the window of the door to the art studio. So many of her sister's ghoulfriends are in that class. Fangelica has an idea. She will surprise them!

Fangelica hides behind a suit of armor and waits. She loves practical jokes. Soon class will be over, and Fangelica is ready to be spooky. Sure enough, the door bursts open.

"Surprise!" shouts Fangelica, jumping out.

"Oh my claws!" yelps Clawdeen Wolf.

Lagoona drops her armful of books.

"I didn't mean to scare you," apologizes Fangelica, helping her pick them up. "I just wanted to have some fun."

"Don't worry, Fangelica. It's proof that you're scary enough for this school," jokes Clawdeen. "But we have to run to Clawculus class. We have a test to ace!"

"And trust me," adds Lagoona, "a test is far scarier than any of your surprises!"

"Wow! A test," says Fangelica. "I've never taken a test. That sounds so exciting."

"It'll be exciting if I get a top spook

score," Clawdeen agrees. "You'll understand soon enough. I have a feeling you'll be at the top of your class, Fangelica."

Fangelica beams. Her sister's ghoulfriends are so nice. She waves good-bye as the ghouls speed down the hallway to their next class, their long tresses flying behind them and their pretty shoes clacking against the stone floors. Fangelica is all on her own again.

Hmmm...Fangelica frowns. She doesn't like being on her own. She spent hundreds of years by herself in a castle! Now that she's at Monster High, she is ready to spend as much time as she can with her new family.

So where is Draculaura when Fangelica needs her?

CHAPTER 2

Let's Scream for Ice Cream

Fangelica sniffs. Something smells delicious! Smoke is wafting down the hall, and she can't wait to investigate.

Mad Science class is under way. Frankie Stein peers over smoking test tubes. Her glasses fog up, and she takes them off to clean them. When she puts them back on, she spots Fangelica peeking in.

"Hey there!" Frankie exclaims. "Have I

filled up the whole school with smoke from my experiment?"

"No! I just came in because I smelled something tasty. I thought someone might be cooking something," admits Fangelica. She loves to cook.

"Really? I guess if you think about it, cooking is kind of like science." Frankie washes a test tube. She pulls a bowl out from under the table. "You learn what happens when certain ingredients mix together, and then all of a sudden you've got magic!"

Fangelica watches as Frankie pours vinegar into the bowl and then adds some baking powder.

Suddenly, the bowl is foaming like a witch's cauldron! Fangelica springs back in surprise.

"Except it's not magic...It's science!"
Frankie grins.

Fangelica smiles and thanks Frankie for
the little-sister cooking lesson. Even though
she isn't big enough for school, she can
learn something new each day at Monster
High. She wants to experiment too!

Fangelica heads to the school kitchen.
She has an idea. She taps on her fangs as she
reads a recipe in the vampire cookbook *Dark
and Delicious Desserts*. This shouldn't be
too hard. She can change the ingredients to
make it vegan so Draculaura will love it. She
pours vanilla into a bat-shaped measuring
spoon. Next she whips up coconut milk
and ice. In no time, Fangelica has invented
vampire vegan vanilla ice cream!

She licks her stirring spoon clean.
Scrumptious! But now she has to put the

recipe to the taste test—and find Draculaura. She puts two big scoops in a waffle cone. Where is her sister? Fangelica hurries out the door, already imagining the two of them sharing a tasty treat. Fangelica can't wait to ask Draculaura about some special vampire tips. She bets Draculaura could help her perfect her vampire handshake. Fangelica flaps her wings in anticipation.

Wow, Fangelica thinks, stealing a lick off the cone, *having a best friend who is* also *your big sister is even more delicious than this dessert!*

CHAPTER 3

The Missing Ingredient

The hallways fill with monsters as school finishes for the day. But now everyone is hurrying to his or her after-school clubs and activities. Fangelica looks at the faces rushing past her. There are ghouls with brown hair, mansters with snakes for hair, and monsters with no hair at all. But nowhere does she see the pink-streaked black hair of her sister. Where is she?

Fangelica looks down at her ice-cream cone. Her creation is melting. She has to find her sister before her ice is mostly cream.

"Mmmmmm?!" a voice rumbles. Fangelica whirls around and sees the big, bouncy belly of Gob rounding the corner.

"Oh no!" Fangelica cries. She cups her hands protectively around the cone. This ice cream is for Draculaura, not Gob.

Quickly, she ducks behind the door of an open coffin locker. Gob bumbles by, sniffing. When the coast is clear, Fangelica heads off in the opposite direction. She hears a strange noise coming from one of the classrooms.

"Woo-woooo-wooo-wooof! Woo-woooo-wooo-wooof! "

Is someone in trouble?

Fangelica bursts through the door, ready for anything, but laughs as soon as she enters.

The werepups are tumbling over one another, yipping and howling. The Werewolf Wrestling Club is having a match.

Barker pins down a werepup brother. He lets loose with another loud victory woof. The pups growl and howl, encouraging him.

"Now, that's a clean finish! Good game!" declares Barker. The two brothers shake paws, friends again. Their tails wag happily. They love to wrestle.

"Are you guys finished yet?" sighs a voice from the corner. Pawla, Clawdeen's little sister, is stringing beads onto a long necklace. She's not interested in the wrestling part of this werewolf club.

"Hey, guys!" Fangelica says as she greets

the werewolves. "Have you seen my big sister, Draculaura?"

"She was just here!" barks one of the werepups. "She refereed our last match."

"Really? Why did she leave?" Fangelica asks. She's surprised to hear that her sister is part of an after-school club. When did Draculaura get so busy?

"I think she had to go to another club meeting," answers Pawla. "Your big sister is so cool. She's part of *every* after-school club. When I'm old enough, I want to be as involved as her in Monster High extra-scarriculars."

"Every club?!" exclaims Fangelica. "How can she do that? Where could she possibly be now?" The ice cream is already melting down her hand! She has to hurry if she wants to reach her sister in time.

"I'm not sure. Can I help you look?"

Pawla asks. But Fangelica is already out the door. Pawla sighs. Her brothers are back to wrestling again.

Disappointed, Pawla returns to her corner to make more jewelry. Maybe she'll design a pair of earrings with little bat beads for Fangelica. She wishes Fangelica were in less of a hurry. Pawla loves her brothers, but she is a little bored of their antics.

It would be fun to do some ghoulish things with a ghoulfriend, she thinks before going back to beading.

CHAPTER 4

In a Pickle

"Ah! Lights off, please!"

"So, so sorry!" apologizes Fangelica. She
blushes as she slams shut the darkroom
door. She's interrupted Frankie and Alivia's
photography club. She doesn't want to
interrupt special sister time! Fangelica knows
how important it is to fang out with your
family. She's so lucky that she has one now!

"I hope I didn't ruin their photo," worries

Fangelica as she continues to look for Draculaura.

Everywhere she goes, someone has *just* seen Draculaura. It seems as if Draculaura is everywhere at once. That is—she is everywhere except where Fangelica is checking. Then she's nowhere to be found.

I better keep checking different clubs, thinks Fangelica. *I know my sister will be helping out some monster somewhere.*

Fangelica peeks into the gym. Bubbles erupt on the pool's surface. She kneels by the water and holds her nose. Then she sticks her head underwater.

Down in the deep end, Lagoona is showing Kelpie how to do backflips. The two aquatic sisters do a series of tricks.

"Hooowww coooool! Haaaave youuu seeeen myyy sisssster?" she gurgles.

Lagoona and Kelpie come up for air. Lagoona shakes out her long golden locks and nods enthusiastically.

"She was just here! She swam a lap with us. Your sister does the best creepstroke I've ever seen," she tells Fangelica. "Do you like swimming too?"

But Fangelica is in too much of a hurry to fang out with Lagoona and Kelpie. She shakes her wet hair in disappointment. Water droplets fly onto her melting ice-cream cone. Time is running out! Will she ever find Draculaura?

Fangelica decides to check outside the castle.

Maybe my sister is practicing flying tricks, she decides. She scans the tennis courts but doesn't see a sign of a stylish

vampire. She spots Abbey Bominable
holding a meeting of her ice-sculpting club.

"Can you cool down my ice cream?" she
asks the ghoul. Abbey nods and happily adds
some ice shavings to Fangelica's melting
dessert.

"Is treat made of...ice?" Abbey asks,
licking her lips. "I love ice."

"Yeah...but it's for my big sister," explains
Fangelica. "By the way—have you seen
Draculaura?"

"Just here," explains Abbey as she goes
back to working on her sculpture. Fangelica
isn't sure what it is supposed to be. As
far as she can tell, it is just a big square
chunk of ice with bat wings that have been
chiseled out of the top.

"Yeah. Draculaura add wings..." Abbey

explains as she sees Fangelica checking them out. "I tell her ice does not have wings! But she did not listen. I tell her I am doing ice sculpture *of* ice and must look real—"

But before Abbey can finish talking, Fangelica is already on her way. She's a vampire on a mission, and she just heard a familiar sound coming from an open window.

It's the voice of her sister, Draculaura, and it's coming from inside the Monster High Creepeteria!

CHAPTER 5

Food for Thought

"Hey, little sister!" Draculaura calls out. She's delighted to see her adopted sister. She waves at Fangelica enthusiastically, but a moment later she covers her mouth and gives a huge yawn. Draculaura is exhausted. Even her pigtails are drooping. She tries to sit up straight.

"Fangelica! Wow! I forgot we were going

to fang out." She puts a hand to her pink-and-black-streaked hair.

Draculaura is seated next to her two best ghoulfriends, Frankie and Clawdeen, and they look worn out too.

"It's okay! It seems as if you're really busy," Fangelica reassures her big sister. She knows that if Draculaura had time they would definitely be doing something fangtastic together.

She looks at her sister's ghoulfriends. They are all as zonked as zombies.

"Draculaura! Frankie! Clawdeen! What's wrong? You ghouls look as if you've been up all day." Fangelica is worried as she slides into a Creepeteria seat across from the older ghouls.

"Don't worry about me!" Draculaura tells her little sister with a weary smile. "I'm just tired because I went to every single Monster High extra-scarricular. As class copresident I feel as if it's my duty to try to attend every club meeting."

"And it seems as if there's a club for every single manster and ghoul," explains Clawdeen, yawning. "There's an activity for every second of the night. The problem is that all the clubs meet at the same time."

"That's why you were everywhere but nowhere I was looking!" Fangelica realizes.

"Really?" Draculaura asks. She wrinkles her brow, worried. "I wish I had a little free time before all my clubs."

"No problem! I just wanted to give you this special treat. It's vegan vanilla ice cream that I made especially for vampires!" Fangelica has been hiding the cone behind her back. She takes it out and holds it up proudly.

But it's too late. The ice cream is more like ice *goo*. It's melted all over Fangelica's hand.

"Oh no! What a disaster!" Fangelica scrambles to keep some of the goo in the cone.

But Draculaura has already taken the cone from her. She is using a spoon to taste the treat.

"*Ooh!* Fangtastic!" she exclaims. "Frankie and Clawdeen, you should really try this. Fangelica is the spookiest chef I've ever met."

Frankie and Clawdeen look at the goo skeptically. But as Draculaura takes another bite, they also try a spoonful of the ice cream. Both ghouls grin and nod.

"Wow! It's like ice cream but soup. It's even *better* than ice cream, actually," Clawdeen decides as she takes another taste.

"It melted on my way here. I'm sorry,"

apologizes Fangelica. She takes her own spoonful and smiles when she realizes that the older ghouls are right. Her ice cream tastes absolutely fangtastic! "I checked in with every single club trying to find you, Draculaura! But you had just left each one before I got there...."

"That's the p-p-p...*prawwwww—*" Draculaura can't hold back an enormous yawn. "Whoosh! Excuse me. I meant 'that's the *problem*!' It's great that everybody has their own passion. But it's really hard when all the clubs meet at the same time. Nobody has time to take a break from their own activities and check out another club. And I don't have time to fang out with my little sister! I wish I had more time for you and Dad."

"But we have to show support for each

club," Frankie reminds Draculaura. "Still, we only get to spend a few minutes in each one. It's no fun and it's super tiring."

"Draculaura insisted we go to Gob's Gourmet Dining Club. But he had eaten up all the snacks before we even got there!" Clawdeen adds.

Fangelica is having trouble understanding the older ghouls' problem. "You guys are so lucky that you get to go to clubs at all!"

"Soon you'll be old enough to join any club you want to." Draculaura pats her little sister on her shoulder encouragingly. "Then we can fang out *and* show support for other monsters' passions and activities."

Fangelica nods, but she is thinking about how embarrassing it was interrupting the clubs earlier when she was searching for her big sister. *I don't think I'll fit in anywhere*, she worries. *I wish there was a club just for vampires. Then I could fang out with Draculaura all the time and we could do vampire things.*

"I wish there was a club where we could do the things I like to do...like flying and bat studies and vampire history," Fangelica says out loud.

The older ghouls exchange looks of concern. Then Draculaura suggests, "All those things sound like fun! But it's *also* fun to try out other monster activities. That's the best part about being copresident. I get to share and learn new things from other monsters."

Fangelica agrees. "Yeah. You're right."

But she isn't really paying attention. Instead, Fangelica is thinking about all the vampire activities she wants to talk about with her big sister.

That's the solution! Fangelica realizes. If she starts her own vampires-only club, then her big sister will be sure to show up. *Then* Fangelica can fang out with her favorite friend again!

CHAPTER 6

A Master Plan

Ugh...Draculaura looks at her schedule
on her iCoffin. She has messages and
reminders from every single Monster High
club. Ari's a capella group performance
is scheduled for the same time as a swim
meet tomorrow. What will she do? How will
she be everywhere at once? When will she
fang out with Fangelica? She yawns. There
is always too much to do at Monster High.

She'll have to figure out the scheduling tomorrow.

Draculaura opens up her vlog account. She looks at the photo she used for her first-ever monster vlog profile picture. In those days she didn't know any other monsters. In the picture, Draculaura looks like the loneliest vampire in the world.

"I would never want to go back!" she says to herself. "That was when it was just me and my dad. We *only* talked about vampire things."

Then she thinks about a little vampire princess living all alone in a faraway castle.

Poor Fangelica... thinks Draculaura. *She was lonely for so long! I don't want her to feel that way again because I'm too busy to fang out.*

Draculaura sits up and turns off her iCoffin. She slips it into the pocket of her pleated skirt. In the Creepeteria, Fangelica looked lonely. But why? There are so many different monsters at Monster High. Is Fangelica having trouble making friends? What can Draculaura do to help her little sister?

"I want Fangelica to learn about all different kinds of monsters and have lots of ghoulfriends," Draculaura says to Webby. He is busy spinning some new cobwebs for the corner of her room. "She's been on her own for so long. I bet it's hard for her to imagine meeting new monsters."

Webby pauses. He swings back and forth thoughtfully. Then he goes back to work. Draculaura gives Webby a thumbs-up. It's good that Webby is spinning more webs— but he doesn't have any advice for her about Fangelica, and Draculaura knows she needs some help. She decides to go find her dad, Dracula, the smartest grown-up she knows.

As she comes close to the library, she hears her dad humming. Piles of books are scattered all over the floor. But she can't see her father. Where is he? Slowly, she picks up the books and follows their trail deep into the Egyptology section of the library.

"Dad?" Draculaura calls. "Ahem, Mr. Dad?"

She hears a scuffle and a sniff. A pair of thick-framed glasses falls from above her and she looks up to see a bat flying in circles.

"What are you doing up there?" she asks.

Dracula flies down to the ground and quickly transforms back into his vampire self.

"You scared me! I thought I was in here all alone. Most of the kids are busy with their after-school clubs, and I thought

I'd have some alone time in the library. I need to prep for my class on the history of pyramid design. And I want to finish studying so I can watch a scary movie with you and Fangelica later."

"Thanks, Dad. But I'll be too busy helping out monster clubs...I really wish I could," responds Draculaura. She picks up a book on pyramids off one of the library shelves.

"What's this? I thought you knew all about pyramids," she notes.

Her dad smiles bashfully. He cleans his glasses on the edge of his vest. "I do! But Cleo is in my class this year, and I want to make sure I have my information straight... or pointed, that is. She's the Monster High decorative pyramid studies expert."

Draculaura can't help laughing. She watches as her father starts to pack up his bag with several ancient scrolls. She hopes he can read hieroglyphs. If he can't, then those scrolls are going to be super confusing.

"What's the matter, Draculaura?" her father asks as they head out of the library together. He can tell something is going on.

"I'm worried about Fangelica," she admits. "I've been too busy to fang out and she seems really lonely. Almost as lonely as she was when I found her in the Van Bat castle! She doesn't have any ghoulfriends her own age. She doesn't know how fun other monsters and monster studies can be. She's only interested in vampire activities."

"What's wrong with vampire activities?" Dracula asks. "Remember she's been alone for a long time. She hasn't had any other vampires to fang out with. Fangelica is probably just excited that you two share vampire scaritage."

"I am too!" Draculaura passionately agrees. "But after-school activities have eaten up my family time. I have to attend *every* monster club meeting."

Dracula nods sympathetically. He knows his oldest daughter would love to spend time with her vampire family if she wasn't so busy.

"I'm not the only ghoul in this school," Draculaura continues. "There are lots of mansters and ghouls who have extra time for Fangelica. I think she will have even more fun if she tries something new."

"Maybe you should help her explore some new interests," suggests Dracula as they arrive at his study. He brushes some dead leaves and twigs off his desk and starts to unpack the scrolls.

"She *does* love to cook," Draculaura realizes. "You should ask her to make you some vegan vanilla ice cream. It is the deadliest and most delicious combination of flavors I've ever encountered." Draculaura taps her fangs with her long painted nails.

"That reminds me!" Dracula pulls a big, dusty book out from underneath the scrolls. "I unearthed these old cookbooks when I was doing research."

Draculaura takes the stack of books in her hands and begins to look at the titles: *Dishes for the Undead, Saucy Spices and Spells, Trickier Treats.*

"Dad! This is amazing!" She flips through one and sees that it includes traditional zombie pastries *and* swamp monster baking techniques. "I've got an idea!"

"Yes?" Dracula adjusts his glasses and

squints down at one of his ancient scrolls. "Can you read hieroglyphs, by the way? It seems as if these scrolls are going to be pretty tricky to decipher..."

"Don't worry, Dad. I'll run it by Cleo when I finally have a chance to see my ghoulfriends," she reassures him. "But listen to this! What if Fangelica made her own club? A baking club? It would attract ghouls and mansters with similar interests but also allow her to experiment with diverse cuisines and cultures."

"I wouldn't mind having an excuse to taste test some of these treats," Dracula notes. "Fangelica's cooking is always amazing."

"Fangtastic! I wonder how I can suggest it to her..."

"How about you leave the books in the

kitchen and let her have the joy of discovering them herself?" proposes Dracula wisely.

"Definitely!" Draculaura is relieved that one of her problems is almost all figured out. If only she can solve her after-school scheduling issues too. What is the recipe for that? She wishes she could just throw all the ingredients together and mix. If she fixed her monster club problem, then she would have time to spend with her newest family member!

All this talk of cooking has made Draculaura hungry too! As she begins to pack up all the cookbooks, she realizes that one of them is giving off puffs of delicious-smelling dust. She inhales.

It smells like cinnamon and powdered sugar and chocolate! Draculaura decides. *I can't wait to see what my little sister will cook up!*

CHAPTER 7

That's the Way the Cookie Crumbles

Fangelica practices turning into a bat for a long time under the fir trees on Monster Hill. But it's lonely practicing all by herself. It reminds her of being back in her old family castle before she knew about Monster High and Draculaura. Finally, she heads back up to the castle. She flaps as a bat, tired. She is trying to pick up the latch to the castle's front door when Pawla gives a bark from behind her.

"You're not going to be able to open the door with wings, silly!"

"Oh!" Fangelica blushes. She realizes she's forgotten to transform back into a vampire. "So embarrassing."

"I think it's pretty cool," Pawla responds. "I wish I could fly. Sometimes being a werewolf can get a little old."

"Definitely," Fangelica answers, but she is distracted. Pawla is holding a steaming Mummy Mocha. It reminds Fangelica of all the goodies she wants to make in the kitchen.

Pawla holds the door open for Fangelica. "Maybe you can show me some in-air tricks? I may not be able to fly, but my brothers have taught me how to do somersaults and backflips. We could play together Friday night when the moon's full."

But when Pawla looks up, she sees that Fangelica didn't even hear her invitation. Fangelica is already heading back to the kitchen.

When she gets there, Fangelica ties on her purple-and-black apron. *I'm all ready*, she thinks. That's when she notices a tower of books stacked on top of her crypt cookie sheets! What a surprise!

"What are these? Books in the kitchen? But this isn't a class..." Fangelica wonders as she pulls a stool over to the counter. She climbs up and begins to check out the books.

No sooner has she put her hand to the front cover of *Dishes for the Undead* than a puff of powdered sugar rises up from the book.

"Achoo!" She sneezes. *"Achoo! Boo! Boo! Achoo!"* She sneezes again.

She holds her nose while she leafs through *Trickier Treats* and *Gobbling Good Goblin Goodies.* "These treats are so tasty I can already smell them."

The best part about the cookbooks is the variety of desserts. These books include vampire delicacies that Fangelica has always wanted to make. But they also include directions that show how to bake up other monster pastries. Fangelica loves a challenge.

Webby swings into the kitchen and lands in the sugar bowl. *"Achoo!"* He sneezes too. When he starts to spin a web, it's covered in sugar!

Fangelica laughs. What a confection! But it also gives her an idea. "We can make edible webs together!" she tells the spider.

Soon Fangelica is surrounded by open cookbooks. She bookmarks a page with a boogeyman brownie recipe. "I hope I can master all these new recipes. Maybe by the time I do, Draculaura will have more free time again. She'll be able to come and fang out while we cook together!"

The idea of cooking *and* fanging out with her older sister is totes exciting. What if Fangelica can combine two of her favorite activities?

Fangelica decides to make some chocolate crypt cookies. She mixes the ingredients and prepares the crypt cookie sheet. Wouldn't it be cool if she had her own club? A club where she could fang out with her sister while trying all these voltageous new recipes?

"Webby? A spoon?" she asks as she adds some chocolate to her bowl.

Webby swings all around. He's spun a big web to hold Fangelica's cooking tools. Spoons and scrapers and whisks and spatulas hang down from the threads as well as measuring cups. There's only one problem: Fangelica can't pull loose the spoon. The web is too sticky.

Fangelica laughs. "Better luck next time! This web is absolutely fangtastic, but it's not super useful in the kitchen."

She snaps a picture with her iCoffin. "How about showing this to Mrs. Wolf instead? It's a great art project! You should help out with her crafts club."

The mention of clubs reminds Fangelica of her sweet idea.

While she waits for her crypt cookies to bake, she pulls out her laptop and boots up the Monster Web. Webby tries to clean the kitchen but only makes his "art project" even more knotted.

Fangelica types away on her laptop.

Trick or treat? What if you didn't have to choose? And you could make tricky treats every day of the week! Come to Fangelica's Batty Bake Club and find out how to bake up yummy monster delicacies.

Fangelica grins and taps on her fangs with a finger before she clicks SAVE on her Fanged Flyer document.

But who does she want to join her club? She hasn't made lots of different monster friends. And it seems as if all the mansters and ghouls have their own clubs already. But Fangelica definitely wants Draculaura to come! She wants her baking club to be all about special sister time.

Instead of sending the flyer to the whole

Monster High e-mail list, Fangelica sends the flyer directly to the inbox of her older sister's vlog. That way Draculaura will know it's extra special, just for them! *I'm worried no one will want to come to my club anyway! No one has time for new clubs anymore*, thinks Fangelica. *Everyone already has their own monster activity.*

As the icon on her screen says SENT, the timer on the oven lets out a banshee scream. Webby screams too, dropping all the utensils and pans he has managed to unstick from the web. They all fall *back* into the web's sticky grip. Fangelica laughs as she opens the oven.

"Here! Catch!" She splits a cookie in half once it's cooled and tosses a piece to Webby. He takes a small bite. Then his eyes go big and he smiles, showing his tiny fangs. The little spider swings from the ceiling to show Fangelica his approval.

"One more won't hurt," she reasons. She puts the rest away to share with her vampire family later. She can hardly contain her excitement as she starts to sweep the kitchen floor.

The sound of an owl hooting comes from her iCoffin. Opening up her e-mail, Fangelica sees that her older sister has replied to her flyer: *Definitely attending!*

Hooray! Fangelica's idea has worked. They are going to have a vampire baking club together. They will make all the most complicated recipes, practice turning into bats, and talk about their favorite vampires from history. It will be the best club ever. It will be *their* club.

CHAPTER 8

Mixing It Up

"...and that's what we think they do with it, but we're not positive," Dracula explains. He's holding up a broom in Humanology class. "But why you would use such a great travel option for cleaning is beyond me."

He can tell that he is losing the attention of his students. It's almost the end of a long day of school at Monster High, and most of the ghouls and mansters are ready to grab a Mummy Mocha at the Coffin Café before heading to their after-school clubs.

"All right, that's all! Next class we'll continue discussing the mystery of Normie cleaning products, including toothpaste," he declares before dismissing the class.

Draculaura waves good-bye to her dad. She heads out the door to the howlway to meet her best ghoulfriends in front of her coffin locker.

"Hey, guys! Are you as excited as I am for the first meeting of Fangelica's baking club? I know it's in a couple of days, but I've got my supplies ready," she says as she opens her locker. There, behind a mess of cobwebs and pink streamers, is her very own set of measuring cups and spoons. She is prepared to cook with her creative little sister. She is so proud of Fangelica for starting such a great club. And she's happy that, even in the midst of her busy schedule, she'll have a moment to see her new sister.

But Frankie is confused. She purses her lips, thinking. Did she miss something? "Baking club? That's a voltageous idea, but I didn't get an invitation...." Frankie scratches her head, and a little spark flickers at her ear.

Clawdeen and Lagoona nod in agreement. What is Draculaura talking about?

"Didn't you all get an invitation in your Monster Web inbox?" Draculaura asks.

The ghouls all shake their heads. They did not.

Lagoona takes out her iCoffin to check her messages again. There's no flyer! Clawdeen checks her inbox. Nothing. Draculaura is the only Monster High student who received Fangelica's invitation.

"What a monster mystery..." muses Draculaura. "I guess Fangelica made a mistake when she was sending out her announcement. I can't forget that she *is* living in a whole new place. We all make mistakes sometimes. "

"But it's a clawesome idea for a club," Clawdeen reassures her friend. "I'd definitely want to join."

"I wonder why she only sent the invitation to me," Draculaura says. "Fangelica is going to be totally on her own in her new club now. Especially when I have to leave early and run to my next club meeting." She puts her hand to her forehead. She feels overwhelmed.

Draculaura's ghoulfriends huddle around her and give her big hugs. There's no need to freak out. They'll solve this problem the way they always do—together.

"*Ouch!* I mean, thanks..." Draculaura exclaims as Frankie accidentally zaps her with some electricity. "You're a little sparky today, Frankie. I'm so worried about Fangelica. Got any bright ideas with all that electricity?"

Frankie thinks for a second and pulls on her fingers. "Here's an idea! You can't bake cookies with just one ingredient. You've got to add sugar and flour and chocolate chips and baking powder all *together*. Fangelica's club has only one ingredient: vampires. We've got to add more sweetness to the mix. What if we all come with you to the club meeting? Maybe Fangelica didn't invite any other monsters because she was nervous no one else would show up. And she didn't want to be disappointed."

"Crikey!" agrees Lagoona. "We've all got to go." She slings her waterproof backpack over her shoulder. She is ready to head to the Creepeteria to pick up some salty snacks.

"Wait!" Draculaura looks down at her iCoffin and pulls up her after-school schedule. "I don't know how we're going to attend *all* the after-school clubs *and* Fangelica's baking club. There are too many clubs. Each time I go to one, another seems to pop up!"

"What if our problem is the *same* as Fangelica's problem?" Frankie asks her ghoulfriends.

"What?"

"Huh?"

"What do you mean?"

The ghouls are confused, but they have a feeling Frankie is onto something, something big.

"Maybe *everyone* is being exclusive," says Frankie. "Every monster at Monster High has their own club now. The sea monsters swim together, the skeletons rattle their bones, the werepups wrestle, and Abbey makes ice sculptures all by herself. Is there any club that *everyone* can belong to? No wonder Fangelica invited only you to her club! I bet she thought no one else would have time to bake with her."

It's totally true! Nobody is trying anything new. Everybody is fanging out with their own kind of monster.

"Maybe the clubs are breaking us apart rather than bringing us together," agrees

Lagoona. "I wonder what activity we can all share?"

"It's just like baking," Frankie thinks out loud as they head to the Creepeteria to pick up some snacks. "We have to find the right recipe so all the ingredients mix together and make something voltageously delicious!"

CHAPTER 9

A Hard Nut to Crack

The Creepeteria is teeming with students. At first this makes Draculaura happy. This is what she has accomplished. She has brought together monsters from all over the world to get to know one another. But now she is seeing something that she has not noticed before—something absolutely terrifying.

"Am I imagining this?" Draculaura asks Clawdeen. "Mansters and ghouls are only sitting with mansters and ghouls who belong to the same club."

"By my paws, you are right," Clawdeen responds. "Cliques are everywhere."

They each pick up a tray loaded with goop and fake-bug gummies.

Draculaura pokes the goop on her plate with a spoon. "We really need Fangelica's culinary talents in the Creepeteria. What kind of monster cuisine is this? Poltergeist pudding?"

Clawdeen looks around the room. She's becoming concerned. Draculaura and all her ghoulfriends like to sit at a different table every day. They want to show that they are friends with everyone. But who should they sit with today?

Something creepy is going on. The rocker monsters are sitting with only other rocker monsters. The werecats are at a table full of other werecats, and it doesn't look as if there is anywhere for Clawdeen and Draculaura to squeeze in.

"Let's see if we can sit with Rayth and his bandmates," suggests Clawdeen.

Draculaura nods in agreement. The two approach the table. They stand there while their manster friends continue to talk.

"The lyrics are the most important part of a song!" Skelly insists. "They're like a body's bones. They give the music form."

"You're totally wrong," Rayth disagrees passionately. "It's the *spirit* of the song that's the most important."

"Hey, guys," Draculaura greets them. "Do you mind if we sit with you?"

All the snakes on Deuce's head begin to

hiss. He looks up at the ghouls and grimaces. "I'm sorry. We're in the middle of preplanning for our first band club meeting."

"Your *what*?" Clawdeen is confused.

"It's a band meeting to talk about our band's club," explains Venus McFlytrap, as if this is the most obvious thing ever.

"Can we join? I love music." Draculaura claps her hands together. "My dad and I used to sing Transylvanian folk songs all the time. Using those melodies could add a really spooky element to your sound."

But Deuce and Skelly are already shaking their heads. One of Deuce's snakes gets stuck in the earhole of Skelly's head and the two thump foreheads together.

"*Ouch! Oof!* I mean, no!" they both say at once.

"Hey, that's a catchy refrain," notices Bonesy. *"Ouch! Ouch! Oof! No!* Kind of skele-punk, right?"

Rayth looks sad, though. He loves fanging out with Clawdeen and doesn't want to upset his friend. "You guys *could* add some really cool sounds. Clawdeen, you could even howl. But we already decided that it could only be original band members in our band club—"

"That's right!" Deuce interjects. "And we have to keep brainstorming lyrics. We want to finish writing our song before we finish our food."

"I don't know why you guys are so worried about lyrics or melody," Bonesy says. "Percussion is the most important part of a song. We just need more rhythm."

He demonstrates his idea by clanking his finger bones against the Creepeteria table.

Skelly starts to bob his skull and even Rayth begins to smile. "That's actually not bad."

Clawdeen and Draculaura exchange knowing looks. They realize the rockers aren't going to let them sit with them *or* join their club!

"I know we're really busy with all our after-school clubs, but I would actually like to be a part of their band," Draculaura says sadly. The two ghouls sit down at an empty table.

"Me too." Clawdeen looks over her shoulder, back at the rockers. Rayth meets her eyes and mouths, *I'm so sorry!*

"These clubs have become way too cliquish!" Draculaura exclaims. "This is a school where every monster is welcome. All the clubs should be welcoming too.

And ghouls should want to try different activities—not just what they are already comfortable doing."

"You should start with Fangelica's baking club," suggests Clawdeen. She takes one of Draculaura's fake gummy bugs and chews it.

"You're right." Draculaura nods. "I'll help Fangelica plan a club that any monster can join. It's going to be so much fun!"

Clawdeen spits out a gummy she was just about to swallow! It isn't a fake bug. It's a real worm mixed in with all the gummy worms. The worm gives a small shriek and wriggles down the table to safety.

"Yikes!" Clawdeen exclaims. "You'd better get baking soon. Monster High desperately needs some tastier treats!"

CHAPTER 10

Variety Is the Spice of Life

"Bat-shaped cakes with fangs made out of coconut flakes!" Fangelica says with excitement. She is holding open one of her recipe books so her older sister can see the illustration of the delicious dessert.

"Yum!" Draculaura smiles. "You know, for my hundredth birthday, Webby and Dad made me a bat-shaped cake. *Ahh*, memories!"

Fangelica keeps listing off the recipes she

wants to try out in her baking club. "I also want to bake cobweb-covered custards."

Draculaura raises her eyebrows. "These are all vampire recipes!"

"Yes!" Fangelica is delighted her sister has noticed the theme. "Vampire treats are the most fun."

"They're definitely delicious," agrees Draculaura. "But I've been eating them my whole afterlife. Don't you want to try something new? Maybe some other monsters will have recipe ideas."

Fangelica blinks. She looks up at her big sister in confusion. "But I thought you might have some special big-sister vampire tips...."

Draculaura chuckles. "Tips? From *me*? I may be older than you, Fangelica, but you're the better baker. My cakes always collapse, and my chocolate pies are more like puddles. You've got all the talent you need to bake up every goodie in these cookbooks."

Fangelica beams. She straightens the purple apron her sister has given her. She thinks the apron might look even better once it's covered with flour, sugar, and sprinkles.

"Thanks, sis! But there are still *lots* of things I don't know," Fangelica admits.

"Why not ask some new friends for help?" suggests Draculaura. Maybe Fangelica can set a good example by getting *all* the mansters and ghouls to join her baking club. She loves fanging out with her sister but she doesn't want to be greedy. Other monsters deserve to taste her sister's delicious desserts! "I'm sure each one of them has their own super-special tricks."

Draculaura begins to put her measuring spoons in her backpack. She needs to head to some of the other clubs now. She isn't going to get more time with Fangelica after all.

"Wait!" Fangelica starts to panic. "What if I'm scared to try something new? Maybe I won't like it! Or maybe it won't like me....I just want to fang out with you!"

Draculaura shakes her head. "I totes understand. But that's not what Monster High is all about! Trust me, just fanging out with other vampires can get deadly boring after a while. Monster High is a place where we learn about the whole world, not just our own. You get to meet friends you wouldn't have found anywhere else."

Fangelica nods as if she understands— but she doesn't. The only thing she hears is that Draculaura doesn't want to spend any more time with her. Draculaura doesn't want to fang out! She doesn't even want to help bake vampire goodies.

I wonder if Draculaura would want to fang out if I baked up a special Danish? wonders Fangelica. She climbs up on her kitchen stool and begins to flip through her other cookbooks. Draculaura was right. A lot of these recipes seem challenging *and* scrumptious.

Fangelica is going to need help, though. Draculaura just suggested she ask her new friends for tips. But *who* are Fangelica's new friends? She only really knows Draculaura.

As Fangelica bookmarks her favorite recipes, she worries that she won't be able to find anyone to join her baking club. It seems as if everybody at Monster High already has a best ghoulfriend and an after-school club! And Fangelica doesn't feel as if she has either.

CHAPTER 11

Not as Easy as Pie

I wonder how my little sister's baking club is going, thinks Draculaura as she dries off with a towel. *I wish I could be there to help out. I've been having such a good time getting to know her.*

Draculaura has just taken a dip in the pool with Lagoona and Kelpie. They are helping her practice her backward boogey stroke. *Every monster should learn how to swim*, thinks Draculaura. *It's so fun.*

She races back to the school kitchen. She hopes Fangelica has invited some new friends to join her club. But when Draculaura arrives, she is disappointed. Fangelica is not fanging out with new friends. She's not even cooking. She is flipping through old cookbooks and she looks sad.

Draculaura doesn't want to scare Fangelica, so she tiptoes away. Maybe she doesn't have friends? How can she help her little sister make some friends? She needs her father's help.

Dracula is in their living room sorting through a big, dusty box of Normie cleaning products.

"A duster!" He chuckles, holding one up. "What a strange concept! I hope I can explain it to my Humanology class tomorrow. Imagine wanting to get *rid* of dust!"

"Achoo!" Draculaura sneezes. Her dad is so surprised that he jumps up and turns into a bat.

"Whoa! Didn't see you there." He flies in a big circle before transforming back into a vampire.

"Maybe Normies dust so they don't sneeze all the time..." suggests Draculaura as her nose tickles.

"Maybe..." Dracula scratches his chin, thinking. What an interesting theory!

But Draculaura has bigger problems to discuss. "Dad, I tried to help Fangelica with her baking club, but she still seems really sad and lonely. What am I doing wrong?"

Before her father can answer her, Draculaura's iCoffin begins buzzing. She has a call. She ignores her phone until it buzzes again! And again!

"Looks as if someone is frightfully popular!" Dracula jokes.

"It's just Clawdeen asking about the baking club," Draculaura explains. Her iCoffin buzzes again. And again. So many messages are coming in!

"And Frankie and Lagoona and Cleo," guesses Dracula.

Draculaura opens her mouth to argue but laughs as she sees her iCoffin messages. Her dad is totally right. All her friends want to meet up at their different after-school clubs. They want to know when she will be coming.

"*That* might be the problem." Dracula puts the Normie cleaning products in a large orange box labeled: HAZARDOUS TO ENVIRONMENT.

"What's the problem?" asks Draculaura. She puts a vacuum cleaner into the box.

"You have a lot of ghoulfriends, Draculaura! You're very social at Monster High. Remember that not only is Fangelica new, she's also younger than everyone else. She doesn't have lots of new friends messaging her iCoffin all the time. She might be worried that no one will want to be part of her new club," Dracula offers.

"You're definitely right, Dad," agrees Draculaura. But it's not just Fangelica. She is also thinking about the cliques in the Creepeteria. No one is joining new clubs or making new friends. Of course Fangelica is worried she might be the only member of her club!

"The same problem is happening in every club," she tells her father. "Every monster has their own super-specific after-school society and never tries anything unexpected."

"Sounds as if figuring out Fangelica's problem with her club will help you understand the bigger issue," Dracula observes.

He lifts the heavy box of cleaning supplies. He wobbles and almost tips over until Webby swings on a string into the room and attaches some webbing to the box. The web sticks to the corners and holds the box up in the air while Dracula gets his footing again. "Thanks, Webby! See, Draculaura? Everyone needs a little help trying something new."

Draculaura is glad she can talk to her dad. She heads to the Coffin Café and orders a Mummy Mocha, hoping it will wake her up enough to think of a good idea.

Just as her Mummy Mocha arrives, she hears someone say her name.

"Draculaura! What's up? I was looking for you!"

Draculaura beams when she sees that it is Clawdeen.

"Here I am!" Draculaura says. She's been so busy lately she's barely been able to catch up with her best ghoulfriend.

Clawdeen quickly pulls a chair up to Draculaura's table and runs her hands through her long brunette curls. "I need your help. I'm a little worried about my sister, Pawla!"

"Really? I can relate. Guess having a little sister *isn't* as easy as pie," realizes

Draculaura. "Fangelica is super lonely in her baking club. What's wrong with Pawla?"

Clawdeen sighs. She orders herself a Crescent Moon Cappuccino. As she waits for her order, she explains her problem to Draculaura.

"Pawla loves our brothers, but I think she's getting a little tired of wereboy time. Our brothers are only interested in wrestling and werepup games. Pawla is a furs-and-frills kind of ghoul."

"And let me guess..." Draculaura smiles sympathetically. "...your brothers are the opposite of fashion focused. They are the messiest, wildest mansters in Monster High!"

"Exactly! Pawla has lots of fun with them. But I know she wants someone to do girly things with, and I can't fang out with her all the time. I'm just too busy! If only she had a ghoulfriend like you..."

Both girls pick up their hot beverages and stare off into the distance.

Then Draculaura stands up so quickly she almost spills her Mummy Mocha!

"That's it! I've got the solution to our sister situation! If *we're* best ghoulfriends, then they can be too! Pawla can join Fangelica's baking club, and the two little sisters can explore new monster activities while making friends! Then no one will be lonely!"

Clawdeen howls in appreciation. Catty Nori, sitting at the table next to them, is startled. She yowls and arches her back.

After Clawdeen and Draculaura get Catty purring again, they knock their cups together in a toast:

"Here's to little-sister friendship!"

CHAPTER 12

Just Desserts

"Sugar, flour, bat butter, baking powder, full-moon white chocolate chips..." Fangelica reads out loud. She is checking to see if she has all the ingredients ready for her first-ever meeting of the Batty Bake Club.

"And spook sprinkles, right?" A voice comes from the doorway. Clawdeen has arrived with her little sister, Pawla. Pawla is carrying jars of icing.

But Fangelica is distracted, looking over the Wolf sisters' heads to the empty howlway. She is waiting for her big sister to show up.

Even so, Pawla is eager to help. She hands everyone a mixing bowl and a set of whisks and spoons.

Draculaura flies through the door a few moments later. She lands on the first row of desks as a bat and quickly transforms back into a vampire.

"Whoa! Sorry I'm late, guys. I just came from the Spectral Singing Sisterhood meeting that Ari, Operetta, and Spectra just started. I never thought of myself as a singer, but they are all really good teachers." Draculaura takes out her own cooking supplies.

"No problem!" Fangelica is happy to see her sister. After all, the club was specially designed for the two of them. "Shall we begin?"

Clawdeen and Draculaura nod.

"Yes, please!" says Pawla.

"I figured we could start with a monster treat we're all familiar with." Fangelica begins passing out recipes to everyone. Webby helped her make copies from her cookbooks. But they are all stuck together.

Pawla reaches up and helps Fangelica unstick the pieces of parchment. Then she looks over the recipe.

"Sundown sundaes! My favorite!" declares Pawla.

"Mine too!" Fangelica says with surprise. "Except mine always end up looking terrible."

"That's not a problem." Pawla grins. "I may not be the best baker, but I've got some decorating skills."

Fangelica and Pawla start to whip the cream, and the older sisters organize the ice cream and toppings. Fangelica giggles with Pawla when the whipped cream gets on Pawla's snout. At first she is worried the Wolf sisters are going to get bored of her baking club and leave. They probably have their own special sister wolf club. But it seems as if they are enjoying mixing up ingredients. Fangelica is having loads of fun with them around.

"Oh no." Fangelica is disappointed when she puts a final dollop of whipped cream on top of her sundae. It's a mess! "My sundae looks like an Abbey Bominable ice sculpture."

"Don't worry," Pawla says to reassure her new friend. "Let me work some wolf magic."

Pawla gets to work. She adds a few sprinkles and puts a pinch of edible glitter onto the sundae. She places a cherry on the very top of the whipped cream.

"Wow!" Fangelica is impressed by Pawla's decorating. "That looks clawesome!"

The two little ghouls take spoons and taste test their creation.

"And dangerously delicious too!" declares Pawla. "We make a great team, Fangelica. You bake up tasty treats, and then I make them look super cute."

"You're right." Fangelica nods in agreement. She helps herself to another generous bite. "I bet we can tackle some of the harder recipes with our teamwork."

The older sisters hang back while Fangelica and Pawla bond over their successful sundae.

Draculaura and Clawdeen exchange their special handshake and a smile.

"Looks as if our sister situation is solved!" whispers Clawdeen.

"Definitely!" Draculaura answers quietly. "Let's give them some space and try to solve our big Monster High club problem. I hope it's as easy a fix as this! Then we can finally fang out with our little sisters."

Clawdeen nods and the two big-sister ghouls slip out the door. They don't want to distract Pawla and Fangelica.

CHAPTER 13

The Joy of Cooking Together

"That was tasty, but I have a secret," admits Pawla as she helps Fangelica clean out the mixing bowls.

"Yeah?" Fangelica asks her new friend.

"I'm still hungry!" Pawla laughs and throws up her paws. "Can we make something else?"

"Well...I did prepare a bunch more recipes just in case we had time." Fangelica is delighted that Pawla is so excited about the baking club.

"*Hmmm*...let's see." Pawla starts to look through the scrolls of recipes that Fangelica has spread out on the front desk. "Bogberry scones? I *think* we have all the ingredients, and I've never tried them! I'd love to make something new...."

"Sounds fangtastic to me!" responds Fangelica as she goes to look for the bag of bogberries. But when she looks around the kitchen, she realizes the most important ingredient of all is missing—her sister, Draculaura!

"Where did she go?" Fangelica cries. She runs to the door and looks down the howlway in both directions.

"Clawdeen mentioned something about Frankie's darkroom club," Pawla answers.

"Our big sisters have a lot of responsibilities! But it's okay. We can have fun without them and still share some leftover scones when they finish with their after-school activities."

Fangelica tries to be understanding, but she is still disappointed. The whole point of her Batty Bake Club was to fang out with Draculaura. And Draculaura is gone. Fangelica is so upset that she isn't even sure she wants to make bogberry scones anymore. She's sure, now that her sister is gone, Pawla will decide to leave too. Then Fangelica will be on her own again!

Pawla decides to distract her new friend.

"Do you know wererecipes?" Pawla asks Fangelica. "I'm not a big baker, but I do have some experience with stage-of-the-moon cookies. My mom always makes them for us when we're feeling down."

Fangelica is disinterested. She half-heartedly stirs some batter in a bowl.

Pawla slowly mixes up some chocolate and vanilla frosting. She wants this to be perfect. Pawla tastes the frosting a couple of times, always adding more sugar. Finally, she nods. She lays out a row of cookies and begins to frost them.

"See?" Pawla points at the cookies when she has finished her decorations. "The white frosting represents the stage of the moon."

Fangelica nods, but she is still staring at an empty muffin tray on the table.

Pawla frowns. How can she cheer up her ghoulfriend? She splits the full-moon cookie in half to share with Fangelica. "This one's my favorite because it reminds me that even though I'm girly, I still have fur and fangs. I can be a member of my brother's Werewolf

Wrestling Club *and* Batty Bake Club. I can do anything!"

"Let's try the bogberry scones," Fangelica finally decides, cheering up a little. Pawla makes sure they have all the ingredients ready.

But Fangelica's wings are still drooping.

"Do you want some help?" Pawla asks. She sees that Fangelica isn't paying attention. She's pouring flour into an overflowing measuring cup.

"Don't worry. I'm okay," insists Fangelica. A second later she accidentally adds a spoonful of vinegar to her baking mix!

"Oh my paws!" cries Pawla as the bowl foams and explodes. The classroom is a mess. Foam and baking powder cover the chairs, desks, and both little ghouls. "This seems more like chemistry class than baking club."

"I can't do anything right!" wails Fangelica. She's so upset she doesn't even brush the baking powder off her face. She sits down and puts her head in her hands. "If I can't even cook scones, how will I ever mix up a magic club so fun that someone will want to be my friend?"

CHAPTER 14

Having a Cake and Eating It Too

"There's the timer!" The oven lets the little ghouls know their treats are ready with a groan. Pawla jumps up and scoops the scones from the oven. They are golden brown. Pawla lifts them out of the baking tray. She arranges them on a coffin-shaped plate. "These look like a spooky success to me!"

Fangelica blinks in astonishment. Ready already? Hadn't they *just* put the scones in the oven? She must have totally zoned out after cleaning up the cooking chaos. But it looks as if Pawla finished up the scones just fine.

Fangelica smiles at her new friend and takes a nibble. "These bogberry scones are so good! I bet they could even breathe life back into a zombie!"

Pawla blushes. "Oh. It's nothing. Just berries and sugar and flour..."

Fangelica finishes her scone and takes another. They are so tasty! She feels sorry that she barely helped Pawla. But it seems as if Pawla has a real knack for baking all on her own. Maybe she could be a *real* ghoulfriend. A baking friend! It doesn't seem as if Pawla is planning on leaving. She's an official Batty Baker.

"Thanks..." Fangelica says shyly. "I'm

really sorry for being sad. I know I haven't been much fun."

"Don't worry about it!" Pawla scoffs as she unties her apron and puts her bangles and rings back on. "I still had a great time. I love fanging out with you *and* trying new monster recipes."

"Definitely! Me too!" agrees Fangelica. "It's scary making new friends, though. It seems as if everybody already has their own friends."

Pawla shakes her head. "Not me! I was feeling pretty tired of my brothers' weregames. But now I've tasted something new and it's clawesome...and delicious!"

"I was too worried about spending time with my big sister, Draculaura, to see that I was missing out on making new friends," realizes Fangelica.

"I totally understand." Pawla nods. "My family is *so* big, and everyone wants to fang out with everyone. I never feel as if I get alone time with my big sister, Clawdeen."

"It's hard when our big sisters have to attend *so* many after-school clubs. They barely have any free time."

"Wait! I've got a scone! A cookie...a...I mean, I've got an idea!"

Fangelica laughs. "What's your idea?"

"Wouldn't it be fangtastic if we figured out a way to include all the Monster High students in *one* activity? If everyone is included, our sisters will definitely come. Then we can meet lots of new monsters *and* fang out with our big sisters."

"That's a completely delicious idea. Hey! It could be a baking party where we cook up all sorts of different monster specialties."

Fangelica claps her hands together and jumps up. She's so thrilled she turns into a bat and swoops a little loop around the classroom!

"Sorry," she apologizes as she lands on the desk next to Pawla and turns back into a vampire. "I couldn't help myself! I'm so excited."

"Me too!" Pawla declares. "But most of all I'm excited for all the cookies and pastries. If you can believe it, I'm still hungry!"

CHAPTER 15

Too Many Cooks?

"Yeti cupcakes…" Pawla taps her claws against a cookie sheet as she looks over a new recipe.

"I found this one in *Warm Recipes for Cold Days*," Fangelica tells her new ghoulfriend. She stayed awake past sunrise in order to scare up the most scrumptious sweets from her cookbooks. She's tired now but prepared for her Batty Bake Club's second meeting. Pawla and Fangelica have decided they want to bake a goodie for every monster. That means they are going to have to learn how to make completely new treats. They are definitely going to need help with the hardest parts.

"Ice-shaving frosting and frozen mocha swirls," reads Fangelica over Pawla's shoulder. "Whoa! This is certainly a tricky treat."

"Yeah." Pawla nods. "We should probably ask someone for help."

"Abbey Bominable will know. She's the head of the ice sculpture club. She knows *everything* about yeti cooking customs," decides Fangelica. The two ghouls head out through the howlways of Monster High to find Abbey.

They find her finishing up another ice sculpture.

"Cool!" both ghouls exclaim as they see that it's a self-portrait of Abbey. It looks just like the snow ghoul.

"Cool is right!" Abbey chisels the finishing touch on the nose. "Cool as ice!"

"Ice. That's actually what we want to talk to you about," Fangelica responds, pulling out the yeti cupcake recipe and handing it to Abbey. "We're planning a baking party for everyone at Monster High. We want to make these goodies as delicious as possible. Can you help?"

Abbey squints down at the recipe. "All wrong. Too much sugar, not enough ice. Where you find silly recipe? This is not *true* yeti recipe. I help you make *authentic* cupcakes like my abominable grandmama used to make."

"Perfect! That's just what we were hoping."

Pawla claps her hands together. "Want to get started?"

Soon the kitchen is filled with monsters cooking up all different kinds of goodies. Every monster has a secret trick or ingredient that makes the treats extra special.

There is only one problem! So many different monsters are cooking at once that there are plenty of mistakes and confusion. Salt and sugar bowls keep getting mixed up.

"What a mess!" cries Fangelica as an underwater upside-down cake falls into a bowl of clawted cream.

"That's amazing!" Pawla insists. "Sometimes accidents are accidentally tasty!"

She shows Fangelica how adding the cream to the cake has made it into a totally unique dish.

"I love it!" decides Fangelica, impressed by her new friend's ability to turn a mistake into an opportunity. "It mixes together a werewolf and sea-monster recipe. It's just like Monster High. All mixed-up and absolutely amazing!"

"Hey, guys. Can I offer my automatic assistance?" a voice calls from the doorway.

Robecca Steam somersaults into the room. She's always showing off her stuntwoman skills, even in school!

"Definitely! We need all the help we can get," the ghouls respond.

"And maybe you can show me how to do a somersault?" asks Fangelica. She is learning all sorts of exciting tricks from her new monster friends.

"Of course. But first let me give you some tips on making the perfect cappuccino. You can't make chocolate crypt cookies without a foamy beverage to dip them in."

Fangelica and Pawla immediately get to work learning from their new friend how to steam milk. Cleo stops by with some mummified meringues.

"Totally delicious!" the friends declare as they give them a taste. "Who knew there are so many yummy monster recipes?"

"I'll show you how to add confectionary hieroglyphs when you're done with your cappuccino class," Cleo promises the little ghouls.

The smell of all the baking goodies drifts into the Monster High howlway. Draculaura and Clawdeen are on their way out of a meeting of Amanita Nightshade's Green Thumb Gardening Club when they catch the smell. Draculaura dusts some dirt from her hands and peeks into the classroom.

"Look!" She calls over Clawdeen. "The baking club is a total success!"

The big sisters spot, through a cloud of sugar and flour and steam, their two sisters giggling over a bowl of poltergeist caramel popcorn balls.

"Wow! I can't wait to taste some of those treats..." Clawdeen says, rubbing her stomach.

"Hold on! We can't have a snack just yet. We've got more problems to solve!" Draculaura reminds her friend. "We've got to check in with all the clubs!"

The two older ghouls head off, happy that their sisters are having such a good time together.

But something very spooky is going on. The classrooms are all empty! Where is everyone? What has happened to all the clubs at Monster High?

"Let's check the Creepeteria," suggests Draculaura.

"I hope everyone's joining one another's clubs and seeing how fun it is to try different things," Clawdeen says optimistically.

But no one is in the Creepeteria.

What has happened? Has something gone wrong?

CHAPTER 16

The Icing on the Cake

"This is too spooky. Even for Monster High," says Draculaura as she paces up and down the empty Creepeteria. No one is here! Even the spiderwebs are empty.

"I think we're going to have to take a break from all these clubs and put on our detective caps," Clawdeen decides after she finishes looking under the last tombstone bench.

Draculaura and Clawdeen head back into

the empty halls of Monster High. There are posters for club meetings on the walls, but no one is anywhere in sight.

"Is it Ghost Gratitude Day and everyone is invisible, or is Monster High monster-less?" whispers Draculaura to her friend.

"Wait! What's that?" Clawdeen clutches at the sleeve of Draculaura's blouse.

It's Ms. Kindergrubber. The ghouls know she is super strict and they freeze in place. Is she going to ask them for a hall pass?

But the strict witch beams at them. Her arms are full of cooking supplies and her kerchief is dusted with sugar and flour.

"Oh, hello, girls! Good to see you."

"Hi, Ms. Kindergrubber!" Draculaura greets her anxiously. "Do you know where everyone is?"

"I thought *you* of all ghouls would

know!" Ms. Kindergrubber laughs. "It's both your sisters who have organized everyone together."

"Really? What are you talking about?" Both Clawdeen and Draculaura are confused.

"The Batty Bake Club of course!" Ms. Kindergrubber is so enthused she almost throws up in the air the bag of flour she's holding. "I was so impressed that I agreed to let them use the Home Ick room for extra cooking during lunch hours. I'm heading to help them right now."

Clawdeen and Draculaura share a surprised look.

"We've got to hurry. Come along! They are baking up a ginormous jack-o'-lantern pie and need more flour for the piecrust," Ms. Kindergrubber calls over her shoulder.

"But what about our mystery of the

missing clubs?" asks Clawdeen as the girls start to follow the Home Ick teacher.

"It won't hurt to ask our sisters for a snack first," Draculaura answers. "Also I'm super curious to see what they've cooked up!"

CHAPTER 17

A Lot on One Plate!

"Is this the Batty Bake Club or a spooky-cool party?" Draculaura asks Clawdeen.

The Home Ick room is completely transformed. There are ghouls and mansters everywhere, and good smells are wafting from bowls and baking sheets.

"I thought Ari had her opera club..." says Clawdeen.

"Look's as if she wants to help out Fangelica," says Draculaura as she watches her spectral friend make tiny white sheets to drape over ghostly lollipops.

"And Rayth! He should be at band practice!" Clawdeen points to the corner of the room where Rayth is singing a song about jam. Alivia and Kelpie keep asking him to re-sing the refrain so they can try to get the recipe right.

"And *that's* where all the spiders were," realizes Draculaura as she spots Webby and a few of his eight-legged friends swinging across the classroom to deliver the correct utensils and spices to different baking operations.

"Ancient Egyptian cinnamon!" Cleo exclaims as she holds up a solid-gold spice shaker. "I can't believe you found this for me!" She happily sprinkles the spice over her mummy wrapped rolls.

"This is total chaos, and it's *totally* clawesome!" Clawdeen says as she tastes a peppermint stick skeleton Skelly has just finished assembling. "Delicious!"

"Fangelica! Fangelica!" Draculaura isn't so sure this is a success. Everything is completely crazy, and her sister can't even hear her over the sound of banging pots and pans and steaming teakettles.

"What's this? Has everyone decided to ditch lunch for dessert?"

The voice belongs to Dracula! He stands in the Home Ick doorway, taking in all the defrightful treats.

But no one can hear him, including Fangelica! She's much too busy taking a batch of merman muffins from the oven.

"Dad! This is out of control!" Draculaura complains to her dad.

"What? A troll? Where?" He ducks and looks behind him.

"Out. Of. Control!" repeats Draculaura. She throws up her hands. "How am I ever going to create a more inclusive monster community if I can't even talk to my little sister?"

CHAPTER 18

A Recipe for Success!

"Don't judge a sweet by its frosting. This
club may look crazy, but have you had a
taste?" Dracula asks his daughter. He hands
her a chocolate crypt cookie. Draculaura
takes it and wonders who had the great idea
to decorate each cookie with a paw print?

While she chews her cookie slowly,
Draculaura takes another look around the
classroom. All the members of the band club

are there. Deuce holds out a drumstick while Ghoulia Yelps spins her phantom fluff candy around it. Kelpie and Lagoona are finishing a tray of deep-sea saltwater taffy. "Will you make these treats look super tasty?" Kelpie asks Pawla.

"Sure thing!" Pawla scatters a pawful of sprinkles onto the taffy.

Even Gob is helping out. He's sitting near the sink, licking clean all the dirty dishes before putting them in the dishwasher. In fact, Draculaura realizes, *all* the Monster High club members are here helping out Fangelica with her Batty Bake Club.

"This club includes every club!" Draculaura cries. And before she knows it she's sitting on the ceiling fan, flapping her bat wings.

"Looks as if someone's batty about the baking club!" Dracula calls up to her.

Draculaura emits a high-pitched squeak!

"Oops!" She lands back on the ground as a vampire again.

"Mystery solved!" Clawdeen has returned with an armful of Luna Mothews's specialty mothball cream puffs. "No one was in the Creepeteria because everybody was helping out here."

"Yes!" Draculaura takes a cream puff from her ghoulfriend. "Isn't it fangtastic that the solution to one of our problems turned out to be the solution to *everything*? Now nobody is being cliquish. Everybody is helping one another out while learning about different monster cultures and cuisines. And our sisters are learning what Monster High is really about: new friends and new ideas!"

CHAPTER 19

With a Cherry on Top!

Cleo passes out sugar cookies in the shape of cats. "We put these in the mummies' secret chamber for protection," she explains. "It's an old Egyptian tradition. Some of the cookies have cinnamon stripes, while others are painted orange with butterscotch frosting."

"History too? I didn't think this day could get any better!" Dracula exclaims as he nibbles one of Cleo's cat cookies.

Fangelica's batty baking bonanza party is in full swing. Ms. Kindergrubber suggests they move the party to the Creepeteria when all the baking is done. Every student arrives with their own special treat.

Each goodie has a different story and tradition attached to it. The baking bonanza is just like Dracula's history class but a whole lot sweeter!

Draculaura is amazed by the assortment of desserts. Now she doesn't have to run around attending different clubs. She can see all her friends in one place! After saying hi to everyone and sampling some sweets, she sits down with Clawdeen.

"What's up?" Clawdeen asks. "Everyone's celebrating, but you look as if you've tasted something sour."

It's totally true. Draculaura is a little sad.

"Don't get me wrong, I'm really happy for Fangelica. But now that she's so busy with her baking club, I feel as if I don't get enough time with my little sister. I miss fanging out!"

The roles have been reversed! Now Fangelica is too busy with her baking club. Draculaura misses her special sister time.

Clawdeen nods sympathetically. "I totally understand. But I've learned a lot from having so many weresiblings. The best way of solving a sibling situation is by having a conversation. Why don't you try talking to Fangelica?"

"That's a pretty good idea, Clawdeen." Draculaura thanks her friend.

She picks up a tray of cobweb candy she had specially prepared for the baking bonanza and heads across the Creepeteria to where her little sister is sitting. Fangelica is organizing all the recipes into one Monster High cookbook.

"I made these special vampire sweets for you," Draculaura says proudly as she holds out the tray to Fangelica. But looking down, she realizes that they have all melted. Her candy is goo!

"Oh, bent bat wings!" she cries. "That's so disappointing!"

Fangelica laughs and pulls a spoon from her apron's pocket. She samples the goo and grins. "Absolutely delectable! Don't worry, Draculaura. Treats taste good no matter how they look. Remember my melted ice cream?"

"You're right, Fangelica. It was so yummy!" Draculaura smiles so wide that all her fangs show. She feels better. "Hey, Fangelica?"

"Yeah?" Fangelica is taking another spoonful of the cobweb candy.

"I didn't mean to leave you alone in your baking club. I totally wanted to fang out. But I also wanted you to make new friends and try new hobbies."

Fangelica's eyes widen and she grins. "It was kind of hard at the beginning. But I'm really glad you helped me see how sweet it is to fang out with other monsters. Pawla is the coolest ghoul ever!"

Draculaura's face falls.

"Other than you, of course! You are the *very* coolest!" Fangelica reassures her older sister.

"Yeah?" Draculaura asks. "I think you are the coolest too. And I'd really like to spend some special sister time with you now that

I don't have to run around attending *every* after-school activity."

"That would make me happier than anything," Fangelica tells Draculaura. "I'd love to learn how to make this cobweb candy."

"Maybe all the sisters can fang out!"

Clawdeen and Pawla walk up to the table. They've brought a plate of half-moon cookies with them. Pawla splits one down the middle and hands half to her new friend.

"Here, try some of Draculaura's cobweb candy!" suggests Fangelica.

The two weregirls share a spoonful.

"Whhhoo-ooo-oooo!" they both howl. Catrine DeMew, snacking on a cream puff nearby, makes a hissing noise.

"Sorry!" the sisters apologize. "This candy is just so scrumptious!"

Draculaura smiles. She put some extra haunted flavoring into it. Draculaura watches everyone at Monster High smiling and snacking together. Even Dracula is sharing a slice of jack-o'-lantern pie with Mrs. Wolf.

"Thanks, ghouls," Pawla says to the sisters. "No matter how crazy our schedules get, let's always make time for one another."

"Definitely!" they all agree. They clink glasses of hot haunted chocolate.

"Everybody's mixed up and it's created the tastiest treat of all: monster community!" declares Fangelica.

Draculaura smiles at her sister. Fangelica doesn't seem sad anymore. She made new friends *and* saved the day.

She has discovered for herself what Monster High is all about!